I0626493

P.S. I Hope This Finds You:
An Epistolary Novella of Love Letters

By Chanel Hardy

©Chanel Hardy 2021
All rights reserved.

No part of this publication may be reproduced, stored in a retrieval system, stored in a database and / or published in any form or by any means, electronic, mechanical, photocopying, recording or otherwise, without the prior written permission of the publisher.

ISBN: 978-1735107363

Hardy Publications
chardypublications.com

"I have written a lot of love letters to the people that I love in my life. It's sweet to be able to keep that, like a tangible letter, and I want to give that to people."
-Lana Condor

P.S I Hope This Finds You

∞*Part One*∞

November 21, 1959

Dear Stranger,

If you're reading this right now, then that means there is a God and he wanted me to find you. Well, not me, but this letter. A letter of inspiration that I hope brings joy to your world. I don't know you. I don't know if you're happy or sad, if your day has been good or bad. if you prayed to God this morning or if you don't pray to God at all. I have no idea what your life is like, but I hope it's a good one. I hope the sun shined for you today. I hope you smiled, and I hope this letter finds you well.

 With Love, Clementine

P.S. If by some strange chance this letter finds you, whoever you are don't be afraid to write back.

Clementine C.

2343 Higgins St.

New York, NY 10029

December 15, 1960

Dear Clementine,

Hello, my name is Daniel Castillo. This will sound crazy, and I
don't even know if you'll get this letter, but I want to thank
you if you do. I found your letter, the one you wrote and put
into that bottle. I was sitting on the beach and saw it
sticking out from beneath the sand. I could see something
inside of it, and curiosity got the best of me. You see, the
day I read your letter was the worst day of my life. My little
brother, only twelve years old, died in a horrible accident. He
was hit by a car that morning, and it was my fault. I wasn't
watching him. I was only gone for a second, and then I heard
his screams. I ran out as quickly as I could. I tried to save
him, but it was too late. Suddenly every breath in my body
had left me. I sat there in the middle of the street, holding
him in my arms. It was so unreal.
I'm sorry, I don't mean to dump all of this on you. You don't
even know me, but I felt that telling you this would help you
understand why I needed to write you back. I was at the
beach that evening because I was going to do something
completely unforgivable to God. I was going to walk right out
into the ocean and swim away, deep and far enough where no
one could save me, like I couldn't save him. That's when I
found your bottle with the letter inside. I sat there in the
sand with tears running down my face and my throat sick with
sobs. All I could think about was my brother, and you were

7

right. I did smile, and the sun did shine that day. I guess it was him telling me that everything would be okay. Anyway, I'm glad your letter found me. I hope mine finds you too.

-Daniel C.

January 8, 1961

Dear Daniel,

I am stricken with so many emotions after reading your letter. I never thought in a million years that anyone would ever find my bottle! It's a family tradition to send out messages in a bottle on our 16th birthdays. My great-grandmother said that it brings good luck. I'm not so sure if that's true, but my mother swore by it. So I did my part and sent positive words out into the world, and by the grace of God, they found you. After all this time. At first, I wasn't sure if I should write back. When my grandmother told me I had a letter, I was confused. I didn't know anyone named Daniel from Florida, but it was addressed to me, so I knew there was no mistake. My eyes grew so wide when I read your letter. I yelled for my father and grandma to come and see. I couldn't believe my eyes. No one in our family had ever gotten a response before. My father was so sure that it was a relative playing a joke on me. But when I read that stuff about your brother, I knew it was real. I'm so terribly sorry to hear about your loss. I can't imagine the pain and guilt you must be going through. It makes me happy to know that you found comfort in my words. I also lost my mother recently, so I can relate to loss. God bless you, Daniel, and may your brother's soul rest in heaven. Life truly works in mysterious ways. I'm glad you chose to live.

With love, Clementine
P.S., I can't believe my bottle made it all the way to Florida. I've always wanted to visit, it sounds lovely. I hope it is.

January 20, 1961

Dear Clementine,

I'm sorry to hear about your mother. I hope you don't mind that I'm writing to you again. Thanking you a second time for your kindness, seems redundant. So instead, I'll say, "Eres un Amor." It means "you are a sweetheart" in Spanish. I can tell from how you write that you radiate joy and compassion whenever you walk into a room. You really do have a way with words. Clementine, that's a beautiful name by the way. What does it mean?

My apologies. I feel like I'm getting ahead of myself. You don't have to answer that or even respond to this letter. It just feels nice to have someone to talk to. Well, write too. My brother was my only sibling, so it's just my parents and me. I have friends at school, but not many. My parents sent me to a school in the Northside, not my kind of crowd. Still, my dad says it'll be good for me. He says guys like us don't have a chance if we aren't educated. He seems to think that surrounding myself with people who speak proper English and have lighter skin will make me into the man he could never be. Still, I have dreams of my own, not that he cares. After my brother died, he wouldn't even look at me. The only time he speaks to me is when he's yelling at me to get him another beer from the fridge.

But that's enough about my problems. I'd love to know more about you. If that's okay. What's New York like? Florida is all right if you like the heat. Do you like the heat Clementine?

11

What else do you like? Inquiring minds would love to know. If you're willing.

-Daniel C.

February 2, 1961

Dear Daniel,

You are quite the gentleman, and to answer your question, yes, I do like the heat. I also love singing and performing songs that my mother wrote for me. It's a shame about your father. I do hope things get better for you. I know how it feels to have parents who don't support your dreams. My father wants me to get a job at a bank or marry a man of good means if all else fails, but I want to sing. my mother was a singer, but my father says ain't no money and dancing around on stage and singing about fairy tales. But they aren't fairytales to me, and they weren't fairy tales to my mother. My mother was actually the one who picked my name. Clementine is a citrus fruit, a kind of orange. But the name also means gentle and merciful. Some people call me Clemmie for short. You can call me Clemmie if you'd like. Assuming you write back, that is. I hope you do. It's been a pleasure communicating with you. as far as New York goes well, it's cold. Very much so. This time of year, at least. I'm longing for summer already.

-Clementine.

P.S., thank you for that Spanish lesson. How do you know Spanish? I think you're a sweetheart too.

February 15, 1961

Dear Clementine,

I know Spanish because I'm Puerto Rican. Are you? My
parents said that there are many of us in New York.
Clemmie. I like that. But I don't mind calling you either one.
It's a fitting name for you. I'm not sure if you knew this, but
Southern Florida is known for growing oranges. I guess it's
just another way the universe works in mysterious ways, and
I think it's cool that you sing. I'm not much of a performer,
but I love to draw. I've been drawing since I was little. I
used to draw little cartoon strips for my brother, but I
haven't drawn much since he died. Whenever I pick up my
pencil, the inspiration to create anything just goes away, but
I'll keep trying. Maybe I can draw something for you. I want
to work in animation after I graduate. I'm applying to an art
school in Massachusetts. My parents want me to be a doctor,
but that's not happening. They just don't know it yet. Are
you still in school? I think you should follow your dreams as a
singer. Life is too short not to do what you want, so sing
away.

-Daniel C.
P.S., I really will draw that picture for you. Eventually. And of
course, I'll write you back how could I not?

February 28, 1961

Dear Daniel,

That sounds lovely! Yes, I am in school, but it's my last year. There are some Puerto Ricans at my school, but they don't talk to us. Harlem is pretty segregated, but everyone minds their own, and we carry on with our daily lives. I'm Black, born and raised in Harlem. Were you born in Puerto Rico? I'd love to see some of your drawings. But I must be honest with you. My father doesn't like that you've been writing to me. He didn't mind after the first letter, but now he's rather concerned. My grandmother thinks you mean well, but my father hasn't been so nice about it. He says I shouldn't be talking to strangers and that it's distracting me from my school work. But I don't find you distracting at all. Not in a bad way, that is.

My father doesn't care about my school work anyway. He just wants me to shower the councilman's son with all of my time and attention. The councilman's son is a lawyer, and he seems to fancy me, so my father thinks he's my ticket to a good stable life. But I think he's a fool who thinks too highly of himself. And he wears plaid. What self-respecting lawyer wears plaid? Well, despite what my father says, I'm going to write to you anyway. My grandmother has been collecting the mail while he's at work, and she's agreed to keep our little pen-pal friendship between us, for now. I can't wait to see your drawing.

-Clementine

March 14, 1961

Dear Clementine,

I was born here in Florida. But my parents moved to the states five years before I was born. My parents wanted to move up north, to the Bronx when they first came here but never got around to it. I was finally able to sketch you something, I hope you like it. I don't mean to cause you any trouble with your dad. Maybe this should be my last letter. I didn't mean to impose on you like this, it was rude of me. But it really has been nice getting to know you. I wish you luck on everything and I agree, no self-respecting man wears plaid. It's hideous. Take care Clemmie.

With Love, Daniel
PS, The sketch is called 'a day at the beach.' I hope you love the palm trees.

A Day At The Beach

By Daniel Santerio
For Clementine
February 1961

March 27, 1961

Dear Daniel,

The drawing was beautiful! You're very talented! I showed my grandmother and she liked it too. I hung it up on my wall, so I can see palm trees every day. Don't worry about my father. He can be a pain, but he can't control everything in my life. You aren't causing me any trouble, really. It's my choice to write to you, and I plan to continue doing so. Besides, I'll be eighteen soon and he won't be able to tell me what to do anymore. Speaking of turning eighteen, remember the councilman's son I told you about? His name is Charles. My parents insisted that I be his date for this political gala. Just to shut them up, I said yes. Well, to my surprise, he's not so bad. And he didn't wear plaid, thank heavens! He wants to take me out again, and I said yes. He also likes to hear me sing. I wish you could hear me sing. You shared your gift with me, I wish I could return the gesture.

How have you been? Did you apply to art school yet? I hope you get in! I know you will. You're too good of an artist for them to turn you down. They'd be missing out.

With Love, Clementine

March 28, 1961

Dear Mother,

It's been a while. I know you're not here with us. But writing to you in my journal is my way of feeling like you're still here with me. I miss you so much. I miss our songs, and watching you play the piano. You haven't been gone that long, but you've missed so much already. I'm finishing school soon, and I'm dating someone. Kind of. His name is Charles. He's a lawyer. But most of all, you missed the most exciting thing. Someone found my bottle! A boy, from Florida!

His name is Daniel, and he's so sweet. A sweet boy whose life is rather tragic. His little brother was killed in an accident, and he blames himself. He was going to kill himself, until he found my letter. I saved him mama, isn't that wonderful? By the grace of God his soul was saved, and I've made a new friend. He's also a really talented artist. He drew me this beautiful picture of the beach. With palm trees! He also called me a sweetheart in Spanish, and I couldn't stop smiling. As you know, I've always wanted to learn another language. Maybe he can teach me more words, and I can become fluent and travel to Spain. I can visit all the places you told me about from your time as a nurse in during the war. Listen to me, dreaming again. But that's what you always taught me to do. I don't know how to do anything else.

With Love, Clemmie

April 12, 1961

Dear Clementine,

I'm glad you liked what I drew for you. It would've been done sooner, but I wanted to add some color. I don't usually color my sketches, but since I've been writing you, it's helped me get through this tough time. Both losing my brother and dealing with my dad. And I felt that my gift to you should reflect that. Something bright and buoyant.
Things here have been okay. Some days are better than others, but most aren't great at all. Things with my dad only seem to be getting worse, and my mom is no help. I don't expect much from her because she's grieving too. But the memories of my brother come back and my whole world just shatters again. I just wish I could talk to him one last time. I'm glad things are going well for you. I know you had to be the prettiest girl at the gala. I don't blame that lawyer for wanting a second date with you. I did apply for art school, but I haven't heard anything back yet. Thanks for having faith in me. It means a lot. And I'd love to hear you sing. Maybe if I'm lucky, I'll get the chance someday. When you're a famous star and performing on TV. Don't forget about me when you make it big.

With Love, Daniel

April 29, 1961

Dear Daniel,

I know grieving is hard, but things will get better. Even if it doesn't feel that way sometimes. Have you tried writing to your brother? I do this with my mother. Whenever I need a way to get my feelings out, I write letters to her in my diary. It helps. You should try it. I'll pray for you Daniel. For your family, for your happiness and strength. For your father's health, and for your art school acceptance. And you can always write to me if you need someone to talk to. God connected us for a reason. I know we've never met, but I want you to know that you'll always have a friend in me.

Also, I've got some news! Charles got me a gig at a nightclub. I can sing in front of an audience. I'm so nervous. I've never sang for anyone other than in the church choir before. But that's different. It'll just be me up there. My face in the spotlight. My father doesn't know, but as long as he knows I'm out with Charles he won't ask too many questions. The club is a secret spot called Lucky's. The owner is a queer man so it's kind of like a hideout for them. People of all races and such go there to have a good time as long as they ain't causing no trouble. Charles says if they like me, I can sing every weekend! Maybe you could stop by on your way to that fancy art school in Massachusetts to hear me sing? I could sing something you like. What's your favorite song?

With Love, Clementine

May 14, 1961

Dear Julian,

Hey little brother, I know it's been some time, but a friend told me that I should try talking to you. she says it'll help me cope with everything that's going on—losing you, dealing with Dad and how I'm going to tell them about art school. Dad's been drinking, and it's getting worse. Every time he looks at me, he sees the boy who let his son die. The grief hangs from his eyes like thick Moss from a dying Willow Tree. Mom misses you so much that she can't even get out of bed most days, but in a strange way, I think it's better when she stays in bed. At least Dad doesn't hit her when she's in bed. He never hit us when you were here, but I guess that's what death does to people. It makes them black-hearted and cold. The only peace he finds is at the bottom of a bottle. Maybe if he and Mom and wrote to you too, they could heal.
I miss you so much, Julian, and I'm so sorry that you had to leave us the way you did. The day you died, I tried to take my life. I couldn't live with what I had done. But a miracle happened when a girl named Clementine floated into my life. Literally. Something about the way she spoke to me save my life. I wrote her back, and we've been exchanging letters ever since. We've never met, but I feel like we have. I feel like she always knows just what to say to lift my spirits. I can almost hear her voice through the pages. I don't even know what she looks like. She's Black, and from Harlem. She loves to sing, and she loved the picture I drew for her. I haven't

drawn anything since you died. Just scribbles of nothing, trying to get back to who I was before. But Clementine inspired me to try, and now I don't ever want to stop.

Until Next Time, Love, Danny

May 14, 1961

Dear Clementine,

I took your advice, and you were right. I wrote to my brother, and it did help. I felt like I could express all these pent-up emotions I have inside. I could get out the apologies I never got a chance to give him. I could get used to this, honestly.

I also drew you another picture. I call this one 'The Blossoming.' I hope you love it. Congratulations on your singing gig. I know you'll do great. The club sounds like a good time. Maybe I will stop by on my way up north if I get into art school. I've always wanted to explore the city. I also applied to art school today, so I'm keeping my fingers crossed. Wish me luck! Well, you already did that, so I'm hoping your positive affirmations get me in. I'm still worried about telling my parents, but I'll cross that bridge when I get to it.

With Love, Daniel S.
P.S., my favorite song is 'I Only Have Eyes for You' by the flamingos. Do you know that one?

The Blossoming
To Clementine
From Daniel
May 1961

May 31, 1961

Dear Daniel,

Your art truly speaks for itself. I don't think I need to
tell you how much I loved it, especially the butterflies.
And I have some fantastic news! The owner of Lucky's
loved my performance! I was so nervous, but once I got
on that stage and the light shined on me, it was like I
was in my own little world. I sang All of Me by Billie
Holiday. The owner was blown away. I had never been
so pleased! Charles says if I keep performing, he's going
to use his father's connections to try and get me a
record deal. My father isn't too thrilled about that idea,
but I have a feeling he'll come around with enough
persuading from Charles.

Things between him and I have been getting kind of
serious. He's been talking about marriage. My daddy
seems happy about the idea, but I don't turn eighteen
until November. With Daddy's blessing, we could get
married sooner. I'm not so sure I want that. But I do
like Charles. I think he'd be a good husband. My
grandmother says that he'll make a good one too, but

she's not as eager to send me off like my daddy is. What do you think?

I'm also glad to hear that you wrote to your brother. I told you that it works. Now you can start to heal, hopefully. And I love the Flamingos! You have good taste, Daniel.

With Love, Clementine

June 25, 1961

Dear Clementine,

I know it's been longer than normal since my last letter. I would've written you sooner, but so much has happened since my last letter and I've needed time to adjust. To start with the good news, I got in to art school! Massachusetts College of Art and Design. I start in the fall, on a full scholarship. They loved my portfolio and my essay. When my acceptance letter came in the mail, I was so nervous my hands were shaking while I opened it. Of course, the happiness soon faded when I realized that I still had to tell my parents about my plans. They still thought that I applied to Stanford, but I lied to them. I waited a couple of days before I broke the news. And still looking back, I think it would've been better if I had just disappeared in the middle of the night without telling them. My father hit me, called me a failure and cursed me in Spanish. My mother cried, and told me that I was throwing my life away. My father swore that he'd kill me before he let me waste my life drawing pictures as a bum. But that wasn't even the worst of it. The thing that truly broke me, was when he told me that he wished it was me that died instead of my brother. My heart shattered and it felt like glass shards pierced my insides. My poor mother, I know she loves me, but even she couldn't take back what he said. The sad part is, I don't even hate him. I can't. Julian wouldn't want me too. I love my parents, even though my father stopped loving me. But sometimes loving people at a distance is what's best.

So, as I write this letter, I'm currently staying at a friend's house before my train leaves for Massachusetts next week. I've been saving money over the past year washing dishes at a local diner, so I'll be fine for a few weeks until I can find a job. My mother also gave me some of her jewelry to pawn for extra money. She's still not happy about me leaving, but at the end of the day, her love for me trumps her hate for my choices. I'm not sure what my life will be like now, or if I'll regret art school, but at the moment, I'm hopeful. And I'm keeping my faith in God. Thanks to you.

Also, this means that I'll be making my way through New York on my way to Massachusetts. I'm gonna stop by Lucky's to hear you sing! I can't believe we'll finally get to meet. I'm excited. I hope you are too.

Love, Daniel

P.S., I don't know much about marriage and relationships, so I can't say if marrying Charles is right for you. But I think when you love someone, you know when they're the one. If you love him, then only you can answer that. See you soon.

July 4, 1961

Dear Mother,

A letter from Daniel came today, and he's coming to Harlem. To see me! When I read it, a strange feeling swept over me. I got nervous. I never thought that this would actually happen. What will we do? What will be talk about? Writing a letter is different, it gives you time to gather your thoughts. But talking in person with someone you've never met before, I'm not sure what to expect of our encounter. I'm excited to meet him, and I'm so glad he got into art school despite his unfortunate circumstances at home. I perform at Lucky's on Friday and Saturday nights, and I'm not sure which day he's coming. I'll have to look extra nice on both days just in case. I wish you were here to watch me at Lucky's and pick out my dresses. You always knew what to wear, and always looked so beautiful when you performed. Charles has been really supportive of my singing career. Sometimes he seems more invested in it than I am. But I guess I should be thankful. He wants to marry me too. I haven't decided yet, but daddy keeps pushing me and reminding me of how well off I'll be if I accept his hand. Why can't we just have fun and worry about marriage later? Like you and daddy did. I like Charles but I'm not sure if I'm ready to make such an important decision. I know that you'd tell me what's best if you could. You always knew what was best for me. I hope I do the right thing.

Love, Clemmie

July 6, 1961

Dear Julian,

I did it. I got into art school. And I finally met her.
Clementine. Before I got to Harlem, I had this image in my
head of what she would look like. But that didn't compare to
what I saw when I set foot in that bar tonight. I got off the
train in Harlem on my way to Massachusetts. There was an ad
in the paper for spare rooms, so I could stay the night and
continue my journey north in the morning. Clementine told me
that she'd be performing at a place called Lucky's. It's kind
of exclusive, so I had to tell the men guarding the door that
I was a friend of hers. She must've told them I was coming
because they didn't give me any trouble, and I went right in.
The lights were dim, smoke filled the room, and I could hear
the soft melody of a woman's voice coming from the stage.
That's when I saw her—standing front and center in the
spotlight. She was wearing a yellow dress with a chestnut
belt that reminded me of sunflowers. The way her brown skin
absorbed the light, it was like she was the sun. You know, how
it rises at dawn over the ocean when the water is still and
calm? That's Clementine. She's the sun. The calm. She's all of
that and more. She's everything.
I knew it was her the moment we laid eyes on each other.
She knew it was me too. She spotted me as I got closer, and
her eyebrows perked up. Her singing slowed down, and my
sudden appearance startled her a bit. But I just gave her a

36

soft smile with a nod, and she continued to sing. She sang 'Please Send Me Someone to Love' by Percy Mayfield, and she owned it. I've never heard a voice so serene and engaging. I never doubted her talent but hearing it in person was such a treat. The audience loved her too. After she finished, the audience applauded, and she went over to the band and whispered something to them. She came back to the center of the stage, and another song began. But not just any song. 'I Only Have Eyes for You' by the Flamingos. My song. She shot me a glance, and I couldn't help but smile. I've never heard anything like it. How did I get so lucky to meet such an amazing girl?

After her set was over, she got off stage and was immediately greeted by a man. Her boyfriend, Charles. He wrapped his arms around her, pulling her in for a hug. He was drunk, but I don't think it bothered her. She said something to him and began to pull his arms, leading him in my direction. She called out my name, throwing her arms over my shoulders in excitement. Her skin was so soft, her hair too. She introduced me as her friend from Florida, reminding him of the letter in the bottle. He just gave a head shake and shook my hand. Another man came up behind him, and he was distracted by whatever else was going on. He gave me a quick 'goodbye' and left with the other man. Clementine rolled her eyes, and I pretended not to notice. She said he was occupied with some other business for the remainder of the evening, so we could have some alone time talking. We sat down at my table, and for a moment, we were both silent. It still felt unreal, being together in person. I could tell she was nervous, fidgeting with the hem of her dress. I tried to hide my anxiety by focusing anywhere other than her eyes. I told her how glad I was to meet finally. And I complimented her on her singing, thanking her for performing my favorite song. She grinned, telling me it was an honor.

I could feel my cheeks burning crimson red. I told her about my trip up north and my plans for starting art school. I got to know more about her family and her life growing up in Harlem. While we got more acquainted with one another, I couldn't help but think about how gorgeous she was. She could see the slowly healing bruise near my eye and asked if I was okay. I said I was fine, and we skipped the subject. I was hoping it would be gone before I saw her, to save me from any embarrassment, but her comforting felt nice. The bands music began to drown our conversation as the people around us became louder, drunk, and obnoxious. She suggested that we go outside where it was quiet. So we did. There was an area out back where you could still hear the music from inside but not as loudly. We sat next to each other on a wooden crate. She reached up to my face, her fingers gently touching the area where my bruise was.

She could sense the solemn in my voice as I told her about the fight with dad. But the more I talked about him, the angrier I got. I needed a distraction and wanted to spend my time enjoying her company, not brooding over our family problems. 'Earth Angel' by the Flamingos began to play from inside, I asked her to dance, and she said yes. So I took her hand, and we danced. Just us, and the music, out in the heat of the night. The entire time, I didn't think about school. I didn't think about money or my parents. I just thought about her, and it was lovely. Before I left, I told her I would write once I arrived and settled in an apartment.

My train leaves for Massachusetts in the morning. I miss mom already, but I had to follow my dreams. You'd be proud of me, little brother. Love you.

Love, Danny

July 6, 1961

Dear Mother,

Oh, what a night it's been. I've been doing so good at Lucky's! You would be proud of me. I wish you could've been there to see me sing tonight. I wore your dress, the yellow one with the brown belt. Grandma found it and let me wear it for good luck. You should've seen me in it. Grandma said I looked just like you, but I could never be as beautiful as you, mama.

Guess who came to see me tonight? Daniel! He got into art school and stopped in Harlem on his way to Massachusetts. I was singing 'Please Send Me Someone to Love' by Percy Mayfield. You used to love that song. Well, while I was performing, I saw a young man getting closer towards the front. I'm not sure how I knew it was him, but when his eyes met mine, a chill coursed through me.

For a moment, I nearly stumbled over my words. I could feel my scalp prickle. Then he gave me a soft smile, and it soothed me. He's such a handsome boy, mama. I can imagine you complimenting his blue eyes.

His smooth dark hair and smooth skin. He's olive-toned like the Latino boys I see at school and in the neighborhood. But I'd never seen a Hispanic boy with blue eyes before. I wonder where he gets them from. If I didn't know he was Puerto Rican, I'd never guess. But that doesn't matter. What matters is how I felt when we talked and when he hugged me. It was different. Not like when Charles hugs me. Daniel's touch is gentle and comforting. When we spoke after my performance, I caught him staring at me. It made me nervous because no one has ever looked at me like that before. He really loved my singing voice. Especially since I sang his favorite song by the Flamingos. You should've seen the look in his eyes while I sang it. He was mesmerized, mama. I remember when you told me about the first time daddy heard you sing, how he had that glint in his eyes. That's what I saw in Daniel's eyes. I learned more about his family, how he grew up, and Puerto Rican culture. I told him about you and how you loved to sing like me. I introduced him to Charles, but he was too busy drunk and gambling his money away to care. Daniel and I went outside to get some privacy, away from the smoke and crowd. He had a bruise on his face

41

and told me about a fight with his father. The pain in his eyes broke my heart. We've been exchanging letters for months, and I feel like I know him on such a deep level. Like we understand each other. But I could tell that discussing his family was upsetting him, so we stopped, and he danced with me. It was such a precious moment. I rested my head on his shoulder, and it was just the two of us. The music, and his hand in mine. He's gone now, leaving for Massachusetts in the morning. He promised to write to me once he gets settled. I hope he does. I can't help but feel like the night ended too soon. I wish we had more time. Even if it was just a minute to say bye to my friend again. He told me his train leaves at ten. Wouldn't it be nice if I could meet him there before it departs? Just to bid him farewell before his journey. But I probably shouldn't. Charles and I have plans to look at homes tomorrow. He wants to buy a new place for us, for after we get married. He hasn't formally proposed yet, and I haven't decided if I'll say yes. But grandma and daddy say it doesn't hurt to start planning for the future. I guess they're right.

Love, Clemmie

July 7, 1961

Dear Mother,

I went to see Daniel. Before his train left this morning. Apart of me wishes I hadn't. Times like this are when I need you the most. To tell me what things mean and why life happens the way it does. Yesterday, Daniel and I were just friends, meeting for the first time. Now, I don't know what to think. About him, about Charles, or anything.

When I arrived at the station, I caught him on the platform a few minutes before his train was scheduled to depart. He was about to board, and I called out to him. His eyes widened, he came over to meet me with his bags in hand. We hugged, and I told him that I just wanted to say bye one last time. I reminded him to write, and of course, he reminded me that it was first on his priority list, his bright smile being the confirmation I needed. He said that it was a real pleasure meeting the girl who saved his life that day on the beach. And that he appreciated my kindness and friendship. I told him that I felt the same and wished him luck in Massachusetts. We hugged one last time, and he boarded the train. I waved as they shouted for the last call for boarding. As I turned to leave the platform, a weight settled on my heart. That's when I heard him call my name. Daniel. I turned back around, a man yelled for him to get back on board before the train left, but Daniel ignored him as he quickly approached me. Suddenly, before I could even get a word out, he pulled me into him and kissed me. His lips touched mine, and it was like time seized us both. Then before I knew it, he was running back to the train and was gone.

I stood on that platform, waiting. For what? I'm not sure. Maybe for the train to come back. Maybe for your spirit to show up and help me process what had just happened. Or for Charles to come and take me away to that fairy tale life in the suburbs that daddy wants me to have so badly. The life that I'm supposed to want as well. But as I stood on that open platform, with Daniel's kiss still lingering on my lips, I no longer knew what I wanted. All I knew was that the boy who just kissed me was on his way to Massachusetts. And so was a piece of my heart. Mama, I need you now more than ever.

Love, Clemmie

July 24, 1961

Dear Clementine,

I hope all is well with you. It's been a rough few weeks for me here in Boston, but I've finally found a job. I'm working in a factory until school starts, and I found a room to rent from a lovely elderly couple until I move into my dorm in September. It's been a struggle, not having my family around, but I know I can make it on my own.

How have you been? I hope your gigs at Lucky's are going well. I'm so glad we were able to meet finally. Although our time together was short, I cherished every moment. I thought about you on my train ride up here. I know you're probably wondering about the kiss. Wondering why I did it. The truth is, I felt something for you the moment I laid eyes on you up on that stage. Something that I believe may or may not have been building up inside me during these past six months, we've been writing to each other. Maybe I'm just impulsive, too caught up in the idea of you. Perhaps I let your kindness get to me, and in turn, developed a misguided sense of those feelings. I'm still figuring it all out. But what I do know is that I didn't want to leave you on that platform with nothing. If we never get the privilege of meeting again, I wanted you to remember me in a way that would stick with the both of us forever.

I know that you belong to Charles, and I meant no disrespect. I wish you both good luck with your marriage, and I hope he makes a decent husband for you. But I don't regret what I did, and I hope you don't regret it either.

Love, Daniel

August 8, 1961

Dear Daniel,

I'm glad to hear that you settled in nicely. I've been quite eager, waiting for your next letter. I checked the mailbox twice a day, every day, to be sure I didn't miss it. I haven't stopped thinking about that day at the train station. After you kissed me, I was stunned. At first, I wasn't sure if any of it was real. It all happened so fast. Then as I watched your train leave, it hit me. This feeling in my gut that wanted you to turn around and come back. It just didn't feel right, kissing and leaving so suddenly like that. I've been trying to keep my emotions at bay, whatever they are. I'd be lying if I said I didn't feel something too, that night we met at Lucky's. I don't want to get ahead of myself because it's inappropriate, and we barely know each other. Do we? I feel a closeness to you, Daniel, that much is true. But how close can two people who've only met once truly be? For what it's worth, I don't regret the kiss either. And I belong to no one, fiancé or no fiancé. I am my own woman.

Until next time,

And yes, there will be a next time. I know it. Stay well,

Daniel.

Love, Clementine

August 9, 1961

Dear Mother,

I finally heard from Daniel. He brought up the kiss, and I'm still not sure how I feel about it. He says that he has feelings for me, in a way I guess. He wasn't exactly clear. Not that I should be concerned. We're just friends, and his kiss was a polite gesture in case we don't get a chance to meet again. Or so he says. I told him that I do care for him, but I left it vague because I don't think we should be crossing any more boundaries. He does not regret the kiss, and neither do I. Anytime I think about it, I smile. Is that bad? It doesn't seem right. Especially when I think about Charles. Who still hasn't proposed yet. But we did find a lovely home in a nice neighborhood on the Upper West Side that we like. It's not ours yet, but he says it will be soon. He hasn't even mentioned marriage in the last few weeks. I'm beginning to think he may have changed his mind. Would it be wrong of me to say that I hope he has? I want to be with Charles, but I'm not ready to be his wife. I'm not sure how I could communicate that to him without it coming off disrespectful. How can a girl love a man and not want his hand in marriage? Is that even possible? I don't even like using the word love, it feels constricting. At least in a romantic way. I feel wonderful things when Charles and I spend time together. But I also felt similar things when I spent time with Daniel. But Daniel and I aren't in love so then what does that make it? And you aren't supposed to feel those things for more than one man, which makes me wonder if love is even real at all.

But enough about boys, I know you wouldn't want me spending all my time worrying about relationships. Not that much else has been happening. I got a job at a local grocery store as a check out girl. It's only temporary so I can help grandma and daddy with the house bills. Charles told me today, that he has someone coming all the way from California to hear me sing at Lucky's! If all goes well, I could get a record deal! Can you picture that? Me, singing on television and hearing my voice on the radio! I could sing on the Ed Sullivan show! I'm excited just thinking about it.

Love, Clemmie

September 30, 1961

Dear Clementine,

I've been so busy with school, that I've hardly had any time
to write. School has been going good, as good as one could
expect. Although having to keep my job at the factory part-
time has made things difficult. I have to maintain good
grades to keep my scholarship, which puts me in a rather
stressful situation of balancing it all. But still, I am grateful
to be here. My roommate is nice, a boy from Ohio. His family
is the affluent type, so we don't have much in common in
regard to upbringing. But he makes for a good friend, and we
have similar tastes in art and music. Besides, that, not much,
at least nothing exciting has been going on here.
I wrote my parents, but I haven't heard back. My only
opportunity to see them anytime soon is the holidays, but I'm
not so sure they'll want me there. Not my father anyway. I'm
not sure what I'll do. I can stay on campus for thanksgiving,
but I can't during Christmas. I'll probably use that time to
travel a bit. Maybe visit Maine or come back to New York.
Speaking of New York, I've missed you. I think about you a
lot, and often wonder what you're up to. I think about our
kiss often as well. I feel some guilt, and again, I'm sorry if I
caused you any trouble over it. I'm glad that our feelings
seem to be somewhat mutual. But again, I don't want to
overstep any boundaries. So we can put what happened that
day behind us, if that is what you want to do.

Until next time, Love, Daniel

October 16, 1961

Dear Daniel,

No one should have to spend the holidays alone. I've asked my father and grandmother if you can join us for Thanksgiving! My grandmother said yes and my father took some convincing but ended up saying yes after my grandmother urged him. He remembered about your little brother and felt bad for saying no. I told him that your relationship with your parents isn't the best and he understood. You can come and stay the night. I hope you don't mind but I understand if you would rather not. It would be really nice to see you again. Charles will be there not that you should worry. He doesn't even remember meeting you at Lucky's but it's probably good that he doesn't. I'm glad that the school has been going well and that you get along with your roommate. I can't wait to see what you've learned and how your work has improved. Even though you're already the best artist I know. As for me, I've gotten a job at a grocery store. Unfortunately, someone was stabbed at Lucky's and the cops shut it down. So no more singing for me.

No one knows when the club will open again, Charles says he can get me Giggs out of their place but I haven't heard anything yet. Still, I'll keep my hopes up. I hope to see you soon!

Love, Clementine

October 29, 1961

Dear Clementine,

Thank you for inviting me. I would love to join you and your family for Thanksgiving. I'll make sure I'm there on the morning of the 24th. I'll try not to be late. I'm sorry to hear about Lucky's. I hope they reopen soon but if not I'm sure you'll find another gig. With Talent like yours anyone would be a fool to say no. I've been sketching things for you between working classes, I hope you like it. This one is an early birthday gift. Can't wait to see you.

Love, Daniel

November 26, 1961

Dear Julian,

Happy Thanksgiving, little brother. Well, it was yesterday, but better late than never. Clementine invited me to spend the holiday with her family. Unfortunately, I haven't heard from mom and dad, so I assumed they didn't want me home. As much as I miss home, this is my life now. I've grown accustomed to being alone. I have Clemmie, but I'm not sure what will come of us if anything ever does. But I miss her already. Too much, and more than I should. My heart pains as I write this, replaying what happened in my mind.

It all started when I arrived in Harlem on Thanksgiving morning. Clementine and her grandmother met me at the train station. When I laid eyes on her, a smile made its way onto my face. She was wearing a green wool jacket, and her hair was pulled up in a neatly wrapped bun. A green, jeweled hairpiece held it together. The sparkle from the brown rim of the hairpiece matched the sparkle in her brown eyes as we greeted each other. I hugged her, wishing her a happy belated birthday. She thanked me for the picture I sent. She said it was her favorite. The memory of our kiss replayed like it was only moments ago, instead of months. The side of her face brushed against mine, and it made me feel warm inside. I could tell by her lingering hold that she was basking in the moment of our hug, just like I was. But we snapped back to reality and didn't want her grandmother to become suspicious of something that wasn't even happening. She was a nice woman, giving me a polite hug and introducing herself. She also gave condolences to my family about you, which was really sweet of her. Clementine drove us back to her house, and as we headed there, I would catch her glance in the rearview mirror. Her grandmother talked about some new pie recipe for dinner that night, but I don't think either of us was listening. We were too busy wondering about our feelings and what the next 24 hours would bring. As we both knew, this façade we were desperately trying to keep up for ourselves, not for each other, wouldn't last long.

Her father wasn't home when we arrived, so she showed me a spare bedroom where I would be sleeping. Her home was lovely. Sandwiched between other rows of houses where people sat on stoops, drinking, playing card games, and just carrying on with their own business. Clementine said that her father would be home from work in a few hours, and Charles would be over in a little while, so we were free to do whatever I wanted. I recommended that we see a bit of the city if it was safe for us to roam around together, of course. But she assured me we'd be fine, as long as I didn't mind any staring. And there was plenty of it, but not as much as we'd get back home in Florida. She recommended Coney Island if I didn't mind the hour trip. We both loved the water, so it seemed like the perfect spot. And it was.

We walked along the boardwalk and rode some of the rides. I had never ridden a roller coaster before, but it was fun. You would've loved it, little brother. My favorite ride was the ferris wheel. Not only because of the fantastic view from the top. But because of the amazing view sitting beside me,

Clemmie. While we sat at the very top, I felt my stomach become heavy as we looked out beyond the skyline at the city. Clementine asked me if I was afraid, and I said no. Smiling, she took hold of my hand, and the heaviness in my stomach went away. Up there, no one could see us. It was like being in our own world—just the two of us and the wind passing by. We looked at each other, neither of us saying a word, and it was like we didn't need to say what was already understood. That's when I kissed her again. Just like the last time, but better and longer. Time was on our side, and every second I spent with her face against mine felt like an eternity. Except, it wasn't. As we slowly made our way to the bottom a few minutes later, we were silent. Things suddenly became awkward. But not in a bad way. We just didn't know where to go from there.

On our way back I decided to break the ice. I told her that I had feelings for her, and she told me that she felt the same. But she wasn't sure if things would work between us, as she still had feelings for Charles. And I still had to go back to Boston for school. Interracial marriage wasn't even legal, which was enough to seal the nail in the coffin of our expectations.

But I assured her that I still wanted to be friends no matter what would come of us no matter what. She agreed. By the time we arrived back at the house, it was almost 4 pm, and her father had just gotten in. I was nervous about meeting him, but Clementine assured me that he would be welcoming. And he was. Greeting me with a handshake, welcoming me to his home, and offering his condolences like Clementine's grandmother did. He asked me about school, and I gave him generic but honest answers. That it was going fine, but nothing special to rave about. He did seem a bit withdrawn, but I assumed it was natural. Since his daughter's boyfriend would be arriving soon, and there was no denying the awkwardness that would be two men, both with close relationships to his daughter under the same roof. And awkward it was.

Charles arrived not long after her father. And to my surprise, he was just as welcoming as the others. Clementine was right; he didn't remember me from that night at Lucky's. Like her father, his demeanor was a bit hard, and he had every right to be so. Charles greeted her with a big hug, planting a big kiss on her mouth as if he had just come home from war. It's natural for a man to assert his dominance when it comes to his woman, and with a girl like Clemmie, I would too. My palms grew sweaty as I thought about what would happen if any of these people found out about Clemmie and me. I hated watching him kiss her. The reality of another man having what I wanted right in front of my eyes made my stomach ache. But it wasn't my place to care. It still didn't erase the discomfort. But unbeknownst to me, that was only the beginning.

At dinner, I talked about growing up in Florida, which her grandmother loved because she spent a short time of her childhood in Jacksonville. I got to know more about the Collins and Clemmie's mother's young years as a singer. The way Clemmie's face lit up when stories about her mother were discussed among her father and grandma, I knew that she wanted nothing more than to be just like her. And she deserved every bit of that same glam and glory that her mother had.

After dinner, Charles told us to all gather in the living room for a surprise. He took hold of Clemmie's hand, professing his love for her. My stomach knotted as I could tell exactly where this was headed. The look on Clemmie's face, the glow in her eyes meant that she did too. Charles got down on one knee and asked her to marry him. With only a second of hesitation, she accepted. And suddenly, as they kissed, the world seemed to shatter around me. Not because I didn't see this coming, but because I had to be here to witness it. To witness the girl I love officially begin her life with another man. Mr. Collins was so happy. You would've thought he won the lottery. We all took turns congratulating them. I hugged Clemmie and hid my sadness behind my smile. I could tell that she felt terrible for me, having to be here for that. But I reassured her with a genuine hug that it was okay. We had already acknowledged that it wouldn't work between us, and I wanted her to be happy.

That night, while I struggled to get to sleep, I heard the door to the bedroom open. It was Clemmie. She snuck in, keeping the light off and tiptoeing to the bed. I asked what she was doing in a whisper, but she just got in bed and cuddled next to me—just laying there, facing me. She fiddled with the engagement ring on her finger, smiling at me. She asked me if I genuinely wanted her to marry Charles, a question that surprised me. I surveyed her expression as I held her hand, admiring the 18k diamond. Something so fancy that I could never give her. I'm not sure what she was expecting me to say and what we would do with whatever answer I gave. So I told her that what happened on the ferris wheel was a mistake and that I didn't romantically have feelings for her. I told her that I let the stress of school and my family cloud my feelings and judgment. Then I apologized. Her eyes became glossy, and she got up and left without saying a word.

My heart shattered. But lying to her was the only way for either of us to move on and forget what could never be. There was no room in my life for her, and she deserved so much better than anything I could ever offer.

The next morning I said my thanks and goodbyes as Clemmie drove me to the station. We didn't say a word to each other in the car, and on the platform, she struggled even to look me in the eye. I couldn't blame her. As my train prepared to board, I hugged her as we said goodbye. I told her I'd miss her and that I'd write, of course. I kept it as friendly as I could. I couldn't fall apart in front of her. I had to let her go. I didn't even wave once I got on the train, and she had already walked away. Now, I feel like I have no one. I guess our father was right. It should've been me who died that day.

Love, Danny

November 26, 1961

Dear Mother,

Charles and I are finally engaged. He proposed after Thanksgiving dinner. It was a beautiful moment, and you'd love my ring. Grandma has already called our cousins and your siblings to tell them about the engagement and making plans for the wedding. You'd think I'd be the happiest woman in the world right now. Except, I'm not. And it's all because of Daniel. I invited him to stay with us for Thanksgiving, and it was a good time. Grandma Gigi loved him, and daddy thought he was nice too. He even got along with Charles, which eased my anxiety about having them both in the same room together.

Thanksgiving morning, grandma rode with me to pick him up from the train station, and I was so nervous. Grandma noticed, but I played it off. I didn't want her asking any uncomfortable questions if she got suspicious of anything. Once he finally arrived, I couldn't hide my excitement. I guess he was too busy to get any haircuts while in school because it was longer than when I last saw him. Past his neck, but not past his shoulders. And it was so slick, but his natural curls showed themselves at the ends. My favorite thing about Daniel has to be his dimples when he smiles. Or even when he's not smiling. Any slight glimpse of upwards movement and they mesmerize me every time. When he hugged me, he smelled so lovely. And his soft, warm skin pressed against my face on that cold platform gave me butterflies. If grandma weren't standing right beside us, I would've hugged him longer.

On the way back home, I could see him eyeing me through the mirror. I couldn't even focus on what grandma was saying because I was too busy wondering how the day would go, and if Daniel and I would have the uncomfortable conversation about the kiss. While we had discussed it in our letters, it was different now. We were face to face, and there was no hiding behind a piece of paper anymore.

Daddy wasn't home yet, so I took Daniel to Coney Island for a few hours. He loved it, and it was his first time riding a rollercoaster. I don't think he enjoyed the ferris wheel at first. He seemed nervous once we got to the top, and it stopped. I held his hand to ease him a bit. But our hand holding turned into something more as I smiled at him, and his eyes fixated on mine. Something about being at the top of the ferris wheel with the cold air stinging my face made me forget about everything. Charles, Lucky's, my crappy job at the store. That's when Daniel leaned in and kissed me. But this time wasn't like our kiss on the platform. This time it was slow and passionate. I could take in every moment of it. His thumb gliding across my cheek, how gentle his lips were. I know I shouldn't have, but I liked it, mama, a lot. As the ferris wheel began to bring us down, we stopped kissing, and the cold air stung my face again. We didn't say anything about it until we got back in the car, where he told me that he had feelings for me. Real feelings. With no reason to lie, I told him that I did too. And if it weren't for my feelings and relationship with Charles, I would've loved to give us a chance. But Daniel had a life too, and it's not like I could marry him one day since it was against the law, so what future would we even have? It was pointless. But we had our friendship, which we agreed was most important.

At least, I thought it was. When Charles proposed, I could see Daniel from the corner of my eye. His feelings were hurt, even though he still congratulated me. That night, I couldn't sleep. I just kept thinking about our time at Coney Island, our conversation in the car, and my first letter. Everything that had led up to this point. I snuck into the spare room where Daniel was and laid with him. If daddy caught us, we'd both be dead. But I didn't care. I want to be with Charles, I really do. But I needed validation from Daniel that I was making the right choice. So I asked him if he wanted me to get married. It was a stupid thing to ask, and I know that now. But I'm glad I did because Daniel told me how he truly felt about me, which was nothing at all. He blamed it all on his mental issues from his home life. Like I was just a mistake that filled a void. Heartbroken, I left and went back to my room. Trying to hold back the tears as my chest pained, but it was no use. I cried, anyway. I brought this on myself.

The next morning I took him to the station and masked my humiliation with silence. It just made our final goodbye even harder. Our hug didn't even feel the same, which canceled any thoughts that maybe he was lying the night before to make things easier for me. But actions always speak louder than words. He said he'd miss me, but I just gave a light smile, and that was it. We'll still be keeping in touch, but a part of me wishes that it didn't have to be like this. You're so lucky, mama. You found daddy and lived happily ever after. I don't even know what mine is supposed to look like. But, at least I'm getting married. Right?

Love, Clemmie

December 15, 1961

Dear Clementine,

It's been a while. I hope you've been well. How has everything been going? Do you have any plans for Christmas and New Years'? Tell Grandma Gigi I said hello. I miss her funny stories. I miss you too, Clementine.

As for me, school has been challenging. I've been struggling to keep up, and the pressure to keep my scholarship has been weighing on me heavily, especially since the anniversary of my brother's death just passed. I still haven't heard from my parents. So I'll be spending the holiday break in Washington DC. I also just realize that today makes it one year since I wrote you the first letter. I still can't believe we've come this far. It's incredible, isn't it? I know you're probably still upset with me because of how things ended when I left. But I want you to know that I never meant to hurt you, and I'm so sorry that I did. I hope that we can see each other again someday. And I hope that you can find it in your heart to forgive me. Merry Christmas and Happy New Year, Clemmie.

Love, Daniel

December 28, 1961

Dear Daniel,

It's good to hear from you. I've been doing alright. I told my grandmother you said hello, and she sends her love as well. We didn't have any big plans for the holidays, except for the usual family gatherings. Washington, DC sounds fun! I hope you enjoy it! I'm sorry that you haven't heard back from your family. In time, I'm sure they'll come around. Speaking of family gatherings, my grandmother knows about us. When I got back home from dropping you off at the train station, she told me I looked tired and asked if I got enough sleep the night before. That question was accompanied by her slight eyebrow-raising that usually meant she knew something she wasn't supposed to know. I tried to pretend I didn't know what she was talking about, but it didn't work. I told her that it wasn't what she thinks, but there was no fooling her. Without asking any questions, she just said that you were a nice boy, and she understood. But also that I should do the right thing. I'm sure she meant marrying Charles, but it doesn't matter. I'm just glad

70

she didn't tell my father. I'm not mad at you, Daniel, so don't be so hard on yourself, and you have nothing to apologize about. I just want us to leave it in the past, where it belongs.

Charles and I have settled on a date for the wedding. It's February 2nd. You're invited. You don't have to, and I'll understand if you don't. But it wouldn't feel right not to offer the invitation, despite our complicated friendship. Also, Charles and I are officially moving in together after Christmas. He brought us a house in the Upper West Side. So no more grocery store for me! He also got me a gig at a new club. It's way fancier than Lucky's too. I'm so happy I can sing again! But nothing is final yet. Wish me luck. I miss you too. Happy New Year.

Love Clemmie,
P.S., here is my new address, and the address along with information for the wedding.

NEW ADDRESS
2343 Canton Rd.
New York, NY 10025

***

WEDDING

Saturday, February 2nd, at 11 am.

New Hope Baptist Church

107 14th st

New York, NY, 10027

January 8, 1962

Dear Julian,

I finally got a letter from Mom a few days ago. Dad is sick. It's colon cancer. She said that he was diagnosed in October, and the doctors caught it too late. So he doesn't have long. He didn't want her to tell me, too stubborn to come to terms with his illness. But after he began to deteriorate, mom contacted me anyway to break the news. She told me to come home if I could. So I ditched my upcoming classes and took the first train to Florida. I know it'll hurt my grades, but that's the least of my worries right now. Mom was happy to see me. It turns out dad told her not to respond to my letters and threw them away. But she kept one of the envelopes so she could have my address. I told her about Clemmie and how I rode my first roller coaster at Coney Island. Dad, on the other hand, was his same old bitter self. Not as aggressive, but still pretty bad. And not drunk, at least. Since he couldn't have alcohol anymore, despite the circumstances, it's nice to be home. Right in time for my nineteenth birthday too. I've missed the warm January weather and the palm trees. I miss all the memories of us having fun. Mom has been coping a little better since your death. Not a day goes by that she doesn't cry. But it's not always sad tears. Sometimes it's happy tears from memories of you—the good times. Dad doesn't speak about you at all, according to her. It's like he'd rather just forget we had a family at all. But mom told me that I'm welcome back home

73

anytime. She misses me so much. I wish dad weren't sick. I know he was horrible to mom and me after you died, but no one deserves to go like this. Not even him. It hurts to see him like this. I wish you were here. I wish Clemmie were here too.

Love, Danny

January 13, 1962

Dear Julian,

Dad died today. It happened this morning, in his sleep. Mom is a wreck, and so am I. We didn't even get a chance to make amends. He's just gone. Mom says she'll be sufficient on her own. One of my aunts just moved here from Puerto Rico, and she's moving in with mom. We're going to say a prayer and release balloons to honor you and Dad's memory before I go back to Boston. At least he has you now. Although he didn't say it, I know dad loved me. Last night, while mom and I helped him to bed, I noticed a picture by his bed. It was a comic strip I drew of you and me playing on the beach when I was eleven. Sometimes, grief does terrible things to people. I'm not excusing how he treated mom and me. Or how he drank himself nearly to death. But I do know that life is hard. And the pain of losing a child was too much for his mind and body to handle. I hope he can finally rest. Take care of him, little brother.

Love, Daniel

January 21, 1962

Dear Clementine,

I wish I could've written to you sooner. But a lot has been going on. My dad passed away from colon cancer. I went back to Florida to help my mom care for him in his final days. It was hard, but we got through it. Congratulations on your new home and your new singing gig. I knew you'd be back at it in no time. I appreciate the wedding invite. Unfortunately, I won't be able to attend. I'm already behind in school, barely passing my classes, and can't take time off to come. But I know you'll look beautiful on your big day because you always do.

I've been thinking about you a lot. After my dad died, I realized that life is too short. Not a day goes by that you don't cross my mind. Not a day goes by that I don't regret not telling you the truth that night. That I didn't want you to go through with it. I lied because it was the right thing to do. Charles can give you everything that you deserve, and that's the life I want for you. I love you, Clementine. I think I've loved you since I found your letter in that bottle. I didn't know you yet, but my soul knew you. And when you responded to my letter, I knew that God was trying to bring us together. And he did. You have a long, fulfilling life ahead of you. A life that I might not be in much longer. But as long as you know that my love for you is real and your love is a gift I will cherish until the end of time, that's enough to get me through each day—no matter where my life takes me.

Mi dulce amor, Clementina.

Love, Daniel

February 3, 1962

Dear Mother,

I'm a married woman now. It was such a wonderful wedding ceremony. The family came from North Carolina, Virginia, and even Charles's relatives from California. You would've loved my dress. It was a dotted tulle dress with a high-neck and ruffled sleeves. The floral embroidery was my favorite part of it. It's a shame I'll only get to wear it once. Just about everyone who you'd expect to show was there. Well, except Daniel. He couldn't make it. Weirdly, I'm relieved. I don't think him being there would've been good for either of us. Things between Daniel and I are complicated enough. Even more so now, because this morning, I got a letter from him. Not even twenty-four hours after Charles and I vowed to love each other forever, till death do us part. Daniel told me the truth. He didn't want me to marry Charles. He did love me, still does, and always will. After reading his letter, there was only one emotion I could muster. Anger.

Not because this letter ironically came a day too late. Not because I regret marrying Charles, because I don't. I'm angry because I allowed my heart to go places it shouldn't have. I kept writing to him when my father told me that I shouldn't. I agreed to meet him that night at Lucky's when I knew meeting in person would cross a boundary I wasn't sure we were ready to cross. I'm angry because I love him too, and there is nothing either of us can do about it.

But it's not just anger. I also feel sad for him. His father just died, school isn't going well, and there was something cryptic about his words toward the end. He said that he doesn't know how much longer he'll be apart of my life. What does he mean? We're still friends, at least I hope so. I don't want to assume the worst, but I couldn't help but think about his first letter to me when he mentioned a suicide attempt. Maybe all of this is getting to him, and he can't handle it. I'm worried, and I don't know what to think now. I don't want him to hurt himself, but what can I do? What if I'm too late? Now I feel like I must contact him, but a letter won't do. I need to go to him. I have his address. I could go to Boston, just to check on him. I can't just sit here, waiting weeks for another letter that might never come.

I'm sure if I told Charles I was worried, he'd assure me that Daniel was alright. But then I'd have to show him the letter, and I can't let him read that. I have to find my way to Boston. Aunt Lori lives in Springfield, which is four hours away from Harlem and three hours away from Boston by train. I could use visiting her as a way to get to Daniel. It's the only way I can see him without it causing any trouble. Charles will be busy with work, so I know he won't mind. I just pray that Daniel is okay.

Love, Clemmie

February 8, 1962

Dear Mother,

Oh, what a day it's been. Firstly, aunt Lori is doing well. She couldn't come to the wedding because of a leg injury but was delighted by my visit. I left a day earlier than what was on my itinerary to make time for Boston and be back home on time.

When I got to Boston, I took a cab to The University of Massachusetts and went to the address from Daniel's letters. When I arrived at his dorm, a boy answered, his roommate. He seemed confused and not too pleased to see a Black person at his door, asking questions about his friend. I guess Daniel never told him about me. Or he did but left out the descriptive details. His friend told me that Daniel dropped out of school a week earlier, and he hadn't seen him since. He did tell me that Daniel still had his job at the factory and told me where it was. So that's where I went. After dealing with more unfriendly white men that didn't want to talk to me, someone notified Daniel that a negro girl was looking for him. When he saw me, it was like he was staring at a ghost. He couldn't believe I was there. But it didn't stop him from greeting me with the biggest, tightest hug that had his coworkers baffled and not in the least bit impressed. But he didn't care, and neither did I. He asked his supervisor for his break earlier than usual and promised to put in an extra hour to make up for the hassle.

We went outside, to a quiet spot to talk, finally. I told him that I needed to see him, to know that he was alright. He assured me that he was. Because of his declining grades, he was going to lose his scholarship. So he left the university. He moved back to the home of the Elderly couple that he rented a room from last summer and plans to stay there until he gets an apartment soon. I told him about the wedding, and how I felt about his letter. He told me that he meant every word of it. Hearing him say that he loved me in person, at that moment, hit harder than reading it in the letter. Hearing it from me, too, had the same effect on him. It didn't change the fact that I was still married. Now we were both standing there, with an invisible brick wall of despair between us. This was goodbye. Neither of us would say it, but we both knew. He told me not to forget about him when I'm famous, and we both shared a lighthearted laugh. He pulled me in for a hug and being in his arms felt just like that night behind Lucky's when we danced together. He placed a soft kiss upon my forehead, and his warmth made me feel so whole. His warmth was all I ever needed, and I wish we had been brave enough to be something. Before it was too late. If only we could go back.

I'm on the train, heading back home now. I have a gig to prepare for tomorrow night.

Until next time, Clemmie.

February 9, 1962

Dear Julian,

Clemmie came from New York to see me. She thought that I was in trouble and was worried about me. I told her I was fine, although she was disappointed to hear that I've left school. She was upset about my letter. Well, not upset, but hurt. She loves me and wishes that things could've been different. But that's on me. I wasted time. I wasted us, and I let a beautiful girl slip through my fingers. This is it for us, and we both understand that our friendship will never be just a friendship as long as we have access to each other. At least I got to hold her in my arms again. You should've seen the look in her eyes. In those eyes, I saw the love of an everlasting heart. They were the wood that could burn with a wild flame yet be forever, perfectly entire. Clemmie is a fire that will burn within my heart for as long as I live. All that will remain when I am gone are the ashes of what I lost when she walked away from me for the last time.

-Danny

∞*Part Two*∞

March 12, 1964

Dear Mother,

Charles and I are finally pregnant! The doctor says my due date is in October. I hope it's a girl. He wants a boy, of course, but we're both happy either way. The morning sickness isn't too bad yet, but I'll have to stop singing at The Red Ruby club soon. Charles says I should be fine for now. If it's a girl, I think I'll name her Sunny if it's a boy, Charles Jr., after his daddy. Charles has been so helpful, making it easier for me to adjust to motherhood. When I'm feeling sick, he drives me around, playing the radio. It comforts me, and I think the baby likes it too. I wish daddy were here to meet his first grandchild. I told Charles that we'd give the baby my father's name as a middle name, and he agrees it's a nice idea. The girl will have yours. Sunny Joline Jackson. That has such a fun ring to it. I can't believe I'll be a mom. I hope I make you proud.

Love, Clemmie

March 14, 1964

Dear Julian,

It's been a while, little brother. I hope you're taking care of dad up in heaven. It feels odd, writing to you again. But something happened recently that brought back old memories, which brought me back to you, well, to my journal. Rebecca and I went to Manhattan to celebrate our first dating anniversary. There was a club there that she told me about, The Red Ruby. One of the best in the city. I hadn't been to New York in a while, so we decided to go. And well, history has a strange way of repeating itself. Performing that night at the Red Ruby was Clementine.

At first, it felt like I was seeing her in a dream. But once she began to sing, there was no denying my reality. It was really her. Standing at the center of the stage, singing a jazz song that wasn't familiar. She was just like I remembered her. Delicate and graceful, owning the room with all eyes on her. She wore a gold sequin dress, and her hair was in a fancy updo. She didn't see me, though. Rebecca and I were at a table on the far left. But I'm glad she didn't notice me. The anticipation of getting to see her afterward was exciting, even though I had no idea what I would even say to her. Or how she would react. Or if she would even want to see me. The last time we saw each other two years ago, we established an unspoken agreement that we would stop writing. After she got married, we knew that keeping in touch would just bring us right back to that moment on the ferris

87

wheel. When it seemed like the world was ours, and it could be the beginning of something real. I had to let her go, so I did. And we never talked again until two days ago.

After her set was finished, I told Rebecca that I was going to the restroom and went to see if I could talk to Clemmie backstage. A man who worked at the club told me that he had to ask Clemmie first. I told him to tell her who I was, and within a minute, he came back with her walking next to him. My palms were sweaty, and my scalp prickled as our eyes met. I couldn't read her expression at first.

Her eyebrows furrowed, her eyes went wide, and then there was that smile. She threw her arms around me, saying my name excitedly. I told her that I didn't know she'd be performing. I was just as surprised as she was. She told me that she performed at the Red Ruby twice a month. What are the odds that she'd be there that night? But I don't question God's timing. He always knows what he's doing.

I suddenly remembered about Rebecca. Clementine seemed genuinely happy for me and asked me to introduce her to Rebecca. We went back to my table, and I introduced Clemmie as an old friend. Rebecca was friendly and surprised that I knew Clemmie. Of course, we chatted a bit, leaving out the part of our past that Rebecca didn't need to know about. Clemmie has been working at the Red Ruby for a year, with other gigs here and there at other clubs, but this one paid the best and was her most popular spot. Then she told me the big news. She was expecting a child. Still happily married to Charles, of course. I'm so happy for her. She's living her dream and starting a beautiful family. Rebecca and I haven't even discussed marriage yet. But I'm sure it's coming. She's thrown small hints, but nothing significant enough to pressure me into popping the question yet. I wasn't in any rush.

Clemmie had one more performance and left us to prepare. Before Rebecca and I left that night, I went to say bye to Clemmie. It was bittersweet. Seeing her again was something I never expected, yet, here we were. Just like that first night, we met at Lucky's. She has a phone at home now, and gave me her number, in case I ever want to call to say hi. I took it since I had gotten a phone not too long ago to keep in touch with mom, who was tired of writing letters. I'm not sure if I'll call. Or even if I should. But just knowing that Clemmie is only a phone call away, after all this time, sparks a joy in me that I haven't felt in a long time.

Love, Danny

March 14, 1964

Dear Mother,

You won't believe who I saw. Daniel! He was at The Red Ruby with his girlfriend. I couldn't believe it! When security told me that someone name Daniel wanted to see me, I thought it was a joke. But they said he was a friend of mine, and I knew it couldn't have been anyone else. When I left my dressing room, there he was. Daniel Castillo, looking at me like he had just discovered a hidden temple or something. His hair was cut, and it aged him a little, but I liked it. It took my mind a few seconds to process what was happening. Then that smile, those dimples. It was like being thrust into the past. I got closer, hugging him as my excitement set in. I asked him what he was doing in Manhattan, and he told me that it was his anniversary with his girlfriend, and they were celebrating. He had no idea that I was performing. Without a second thought, I told him to introduce me to her. She was friendly and gorgeous, too, with chestnut brown hair and an olive skin tone like him. Latino, I assumed.

We sat at his table and talked about what the other had been up to these past few years. I told him about my father's passing, and he gave his condolences. He was living in New Jersey now, illustrating for a publication that made comics. His friend from college got him a job, and he enjoys it. Although he still has plans to go back to school and finish his degree. I shared the news that Charles and I were having a baby. He seemed happy for me, but why wouldn't he be? Daniel has always been kind and supportive, and I didn't expect that anything had changed. Despite our history. Before they left that night, I told him how great it was that we got to see each other again. I gave him my number, in case he ever wants to catch up again. I'm not sure if he'll bother, and that's okay. But I hope he does. His friendship meant a lot to me, even if it had to end out of respect for my marriage. I did send him a Christmas card that same year, but it was sent back. I guess he had moved. I took it as a sign and never attempted to contact him after that. But now, my friend is back. Well, not really. But the window is there. It's up to him if he wants to climb through it or not. Only time will tell.

Love, Clemmie

April 21, 1964

Dear Mother,

Daniel called me today. It was so strange, talking to him over the phone. But it was nice to hear his voice again. He just wanted to say hello and tell me that he would be back in New York on a business trip next week. He asked if I wanted to go out to lunch to talk. With just us this time. He would be alone, so either of us wouldn't have to walk on eggshells or worry about slipping up and saying something that would make his girlfriend uncomfortable. I was hesitant. After all, we had just seen each other at The Red Ruby. But he said that he doesn't know when he'll be back in New York, and Charles has been considering a move out west. For all we know, this could be my last chance to see Daniel. Even though we caught up nicely the last time, he did have a point about us not getting an opportunity to take our time and talk how we wanted to. So, I said yes. We're meeting at a café in my neighborhood. The best part is, I don't have to lie to Charles about it. I told him about our little reunion and that Daniel has a girlfriend. To soften it up.

To be honest, I'm not looking forward to this move to California. With the baby coming, I want to stay close to grandma, and she'd never leave Harlem. If daddy were still here, it would be different. But I'm all she has now.

I told Charles that I'm not leaving until the baby is born if we have to go. I want to have it here. No matter what he says.

Love, Clemmie

April 28, 1964

Dear Julian,

After spending weeks contemplating, I finally gave
Clementine a call. I was so nervous because talking on the
phone isn't like writing a letter. And I wasn't sure if her
husband would pick up, which would've been a little awkward.
I told her that I would be in New York on business and
wanted another opportunity to see her. She said yes, so we
met at a little café in her old neighborhood. I also got to stop
by her old home to say hello to grandma Gigi, who was as
delightful as always. Clemmie asked if Rebecca and I were
planning on getting married and having any children. I said no,
but it wasn't off the table for me. She asked about how
Rebecca and I met, but I wasn't there to talk about Rebecca.
I was there to talk about us.
The truth is, my life began to spiral into a dark place after
Clemmie left. I lost my job at the factory and began to drink
a lot. That's how I ended up meeting Rebecca. Her dad ran a
restaurant in Medford, and I got a job washing dishes. That's
how I ended up running into my old roommate, who put in a
good word for me in Jersey. When I got my illustrating job,
Rebecca agreed to go with me to Jersey, and we've been
together since. So many times, I wanted to write to Clemmie
but never could. She never wrote to me, so I figured she
wouldn't respond even if I could get up the courage to form
anything more than a sentence. I told Clemmie all of this, and
she said she would've written me back if I had. She told me

she mailed a Christmas card that I never got and still thought about me from time to time. She told me she still had my pictures and shared a funny story about going to Coney Island with Charles and pretending to be too sick for the ferris wheel. We shared a laugh that left me feeling a bit out of sorts. Her, also, as our moment of amusement, turned into an awkward silence. This is why I wanted us to be alone. We couldn't have had this kind of conversation that night at the club with Rebecca sitting next to me. A conversation that awakened old wounds and lingering what-ifs.

I skipped the subject and asked her about her upcoming addition to the family. She told me that she was nervous about becoming a mom and that her husband wanted to move to California. My stomach turned at the thought of her being so far away after she just came back into my life. Now I was feeling guilt from my selfishness. She wasn't in my life anymore, and it wasn't my place to feel any kind of way about hers. She reached across the table, placing her hand on mine. She gave me that beautiful smile that I love so much, and told me to make a bunch of cute babies with my girl and to stay well. I promised her I would, still clinging on to her hand. Still clinging on to the memory of what her soft fingers felt like after she left.

It's a good thing you don't have to worry about me teaching you about love and relationships like older brothers are supposed to, because clearly, I'm no good at it.

Love, Danny

October 2, 1964

Dear Julian,

The only time I ever remember praying, like really praying, was when I found you outside that day. I prayed for God to let you live, and when he didn't, I lost all hope in him ever doing anything for me. But as I sit in this hospital room, next to Clemmie, I know that God does hear us, and he was listening when I prayed for her.

A few days ago, I called Clemmie to check on her since I knew her baby would be due any day now. I didn't get an answer, but something in me told me to call back. I'm not sure what it was, but I'm glad I did. On the second call, her grandmother answered. There was solemn in her voice, and I knew something was wrong because she didn't live with Clemmie. She told me that Clemmie had been hurt and was in the hospital. She was stabbed. My heart sank into my stomach. I tried to get more out of her, but she could hardly get any details out. She told me which hospital Clemmie was admitted to, and without giving it another thought, I drove overnight to New York. During the drive, I prayed for Clemmie's recovery and her baby. Not knowing what exactly happened or if she was still alive was eating away at me. I kept wondering what kind of monster would hurt her? Who would do something so terrible to a pregnant woman, and why her? I was furious, hurt, so many emotions went through me

P.S I Hope This Finds You

that I couldn't even focus on driving the majority of the way there.

When I arrived, I was given Clemmie's room number, where Grandma Gigi was sitting at her bedside. She greeted me with a hug, surprised to see me there so soon. Clemmie was alive, so was the baby. She was sleeping when I got there but was doing okay. According to Grandma Gigi, Clemmie and Charles had been the victims of an attack.

Someone had broken into their home in what appeared to be a burglary. Both Clemmie and Charles were stabbed. Unfortunately, Charles didn't survive. Clemmie had enough strength to reach the phone and call 911. She was unconscious by the time the medics arrived, but they were able to save her, and she was able to have a safe delivery—a beautiful baby girl named Sunny Joline. Grandma Gigi also said that rumors are going around that Charles was involved in some messy business. He owed a gambling debt, and the men wanted their money no matter what it cost, even if it cost him, his wife, and their unborn child their lives.

My eyes filled with tears as I walked over to Clemmie's bed and held her hand. The thought of losing her was too much to process. And now, she has to deal with being a new mother and a widow. I hate that she has to go through this, but by the grace of God, Clemmie and her baby are alive. And that's all that matters now.

Love, Danny

October 5, 1964

Dear Mother,

Sunny Joline Jackson. Sunny Jo, for short, was born at
2:32 am at Mercy Hospital. She's so beautiful, and
you'd love her. Grandma sure does. She says Sunny looks
just like me, but I think she looks like Charles' mother.
Sunny has their eyes, that's for sure. I only wish that
she could meet her daddy, but God had other plans. I'm
not sure how I have the emotional strength to write
this. To tell you about what happened to us. I won't go
into details because that would require living through it
again, and I don't want to do that. I don't want to
suffer any more than I am already suffering. Charles is
gone, and I don't know how I'll ever go on without him.
How will I raise Sunny alone? How will I explain to her
that her father was a troubled man that led to his
death? I blame myself partially. I knew something was
going on with him, but he brushed them off anytime I
asked questions and told me it was nothing. But it
wasn't nothing. He owed people money, and this is why

he wanted to move to California so badly. Maybe if I weren't so adamant about waiting, we'd be across the country by now, and my daughter would still have a father. Daniel tells me not to blame myself, and I know he's right. But that doesn't change the fact that I could've done something. I still have to live with that. But I'm just thankful that I'm here, and I have Sunny now.

Speaking of Daniel, he drove all the way here in the middle of the night to come to see me in the hospital. When I woke up, seeing him was a pleasant surprise, and honestly, I needed the comfort of a friend by my side. I told him that he didn't have to come all the way here, but he insisted that he did. Charles's funeral is this Saturday, and I'm not looking forward to it. You know that I've never liked funerals, but life must go on. Daniel said he would attend if he could, but he had to get back to New Jersey for work. He sent flowers, beautiful ones, and told me to call him if I need anything.

Sunny and I are out of the hospital now. After my surgery and some rest, the doctors said I could go home. I'm selling our home and moving back to Harlem with Grandma. I got money from Charles's insurance policy, so I'm putting it aside until I can find work and carry out on my own again. Daddy's house is paid off now, so Sunny, Grandma, and I should be fine. I could use the help with a newborn and all. It will take some time, but I'll get through this. I'll be okay.

Love, Clemmie

November 16, 1964

Dear Julian,

I'm back in New York again. A week ago, Clemmie called me, crying. She was having a hard time with Sunny, and her grandmother left to help care for a sick relative in Virginia. One of Clemmie's cousins came for a few days but couldn't stay. She just needed someone to talk to, but I offered to help out instead since I had the free time. And since Rebecca and I are no longer together. I still haven't told Clemmie why, and I'm not sure I'm ready to. I just realized I haven't even shared the news with you.

I've enlisted in the Military. The Marines, to be exact. In three weeks, I'll be leaving for Fort Polk, Louisiana. After my basic training, I'll be shipping out to Ho Chi Minh, Vietnam. I know it sounds crazy, me being a soldier. Three years ago, I would've said the same. But the G.I. Bill can pay for my education. It's the only way I can go back to finish my degree. Mom wasn't too happy with my decision. Neither was Rebecca. She ended our relationship because the thought of me dying in some war was too much for her. She couldn't wait around for me, and I'm not going to hold that against her. I'm not sure I would wait for me either.

Sunny is a joy to be around. She looks just like Clemmie, especially when she smiles. I'm glad that I could help out and give Clemmie a break she so desperately needs. She's delighted to have me around too. When the baby is sleeping, we get to spend some quality time together. Listening to music and watching her favorite shows. I hate that it's only temporary. At first, I felt guilty, enjoying this time with her. It's only been almost 2 months since her husband's passing, and I don't want any of this to come off wrong. But she said it's okay. She appreciates the company and said she'd rather it be me than her mother-in-law or one of her judgy cousins. She called Grandma Gigi to tell her I was here, and she doesn't seem to mind either. It's nice being with Clemmie again and watching her grow into this sweet, nurturing, delicate mother. I hope God continues to bless her. She deserves the world.

Love, Your future soldier brother, Danny

November 21, 1964

Dear Mother,

You know how you used to say, when God closes one door, he opens another? You weren't wrong. God closed a door when he took Charles away. But he opened a new door when Daniel came from New Jersey to help with Sunny. I can't even call it a new door with Daniel because his door to my life never truly left. It's always been there, cracked open a little and waiting for God to push it open again.

As you know, it's my 21st birthday. Another year older, but I'm blessed with a daughter to share it with now. Grandma Gigi came back from Virginia yesterday, which was perfect timing because she offered to watch Sunny while Daniel and I went to Coney Island to celebrate. It was his idea, and you know I couldn't resist a day at Coney. We had such a wonderful time. We even rode the Ferris wheel again. But my joy of spending my birthday with my best friend was cut short when that door God opened, slammed closed, right in my face again. At the top of the ferris wheel, Daniel told me

that he enlisted in the Military and is going to Vietnam.
A chill hit me like ice water, and it wasn't because of
the wind. My heart broke for him. He says he did it to
pay for school, but no education is worth your life. He
tells me not to worry. He has faith and only asks that I
pray for him. Which I will. I don't want him to go. I
don't want him to die; I can't lose anyone else that I
love. Not now. But it's too late. He's leaving in the
morning and going to visit his mother before he goes to
Basic training.

There is something else I want to tell you because I
know you raised me to be a woman of God. But women
of God don't commit adultery, even if their husband is
deceased. Even if the man they love is about to go off on
a suicide mission for the government. But I'm not a
woman of God anymore. I'm a woman of my own, who
follows God's wisdom but refuses to let it hinder my life.
I had sex with Daniel. I shared a part of myself with
him that I never imagined I would, and it was beautiful.
I don't regret what we did tonight, and neither does he.
It wasn't a coincidence that his ex-girlfriend chose The
Red Ruby that night. It's no coincidence that I begged
Charles to hold off on our move to California. And it's

no coincidence that God brought Daniel and me back together again. I love him. I always have, and despite the future that awaits him when he leaves for Vietnam, I wanted him to know just how much I've always loved him. Just in case I never see him again.

Love, Clemmie

November 22, 1964

Dear Julian,

I'm on my way to Florida to see mom before I go. I don't know what kind of life awaits me when I get to Louisiana or Vietnam. But I do know that I'll be leaving behind no regrets. Telling Clemmie was one of the hardest things I've ever had to do. Seeing the look of shock, worry, and disappointment on her face was painful. At least we got to spend our last day together at her favorite place. Since Clemmie and I reunited back in March, I never once asked her if she still loved me. She never asked me either. But when I rushed to be with her at the hospital that day, I think we both knew that there was no denying it. And last night, she made that clear. I thought back to Thanksgiving in '61 when she came to my room that night and laid next to me, asking about her decision to marry. That should've been my moment, to be honest, and I pushed her away instead. But this time when she came to my bed, I didn't push her away. Clemmie, and me, we are one now. I'll spare you the details, little brother, but know that I'll be going to fight this war with a piece of Clemmie's heart & soul with me. Saying goodbye this morning was rough for both of us, but we remained firm. She prayed for me, so did Grandma Gigi, and I went on my way. The reality of possibly never seeing her again didn't hit until I left, and it left my heart shattered in disarray. There were things in my life that I was never ashamed of giving up. But Clemmie wasn't one of them. As I said, I have no regrets about joining the Military to better my life and serve my country. I have no regrets about leaving Florida to chase my dreams, and I have no regrets about falling in love. I hope Clemmie never forgets me. I'll always remember her.

Love, Danny

∞*Part Three*∞

February 3, 1965

Dear Mother,

I saw the doctor today because I haven't been feeling well. I figured it was just stress from keeping up with Sunny all hours of the day. But I was in for a rather big surprise. I'm nine weeks pregnant with Daniel's child. I haven't told Grandma yet. I'm still coming down from my high of emotions, which are a mix of fear, joy, and unease. I think she already suspects it but wants to wait until I bring it up first. Then I have to tell Daniel, who is already on his way to Vietnam. The last time I spoke to him was when he called me from Louisiana a week ago. I would've mentioned it then, but it was a short call, and I wasn't sure yet, and more so thought it was just a bug going around. I didn't want him distracted over something that turned out to be nothing. What am I going to do with two babies by myself? Especially if Daniel perishes at war. Oh, the irony that is us.

Love, Clemmie

March 30, 1965

Dear Clemmie,

I miss you so much already. It's such a culture shock being in
a different country, and much hotter than what I was used
to growing up in Florida. You'd be pleased to know that I was
one of the top, outstanding graduates in my brigade at Basic.
My mother will be proud when I tell her. It'll give her
something to be hopeful about while I'm here.
How are things at home? I hope Sunny isn't giving you too
much of a hard time. Tell Grandma Gigi I said hello. I hope
you're not worrying too much. I've been fine so far. They sent
my squad directly into combat, our first mission being a
Sunday morning. Everything went smoothly at first until we
started to level out. Our first target was a group scattered
down in the fields below. As we prepared to drop down, I saw
something emerge. Something big and dark that turned red.
It was a fire. I and a few others headed in the opposite
direction, while others went forward. We had to spread out.
Thankfully, my squad and I survived to fight another day.
With only two men wounded. But I'm sure you don't want to
hear about the traumas of war in all of my letters, so I'll try
my best to not talk about the bad things. Only good things.
Like memories of us or fascinating things about Saigon. I
can't wait to hear from you. Love you and miss you.

Love, Danny.
P.S., I drew a little something for you.

April 22, 1965

Dear Daniel,

I still can't believe you're out there. It makes me happy to know that you're okay. We're fine here, and Sunny has been her usual, jolly self. The picture was beautiful. Thank you for that. I won't beat around the bush. There's something that you need to know. I'm pregnant. You're going to be a father. I found out at the beginning of February, right after you left. I wish I had found out sooner, and I hate that you have to find out this way. My grandma isn't too happy about the circumstances. She thinks it's too soon for me to be having another child, out of wedlock at that. But she says a baby is a blessing regardless. Even though she won't show it, I know she's excited. I am too. Afraid, but I love them already. I'm due in August. A summer baby. If it's a girl, I think I'll name her Sky. If it's a boy, he'll be named after you unless you have another name in mind. I'll let you decide.

Since there's a new baby on the way, I'm staying with Grandma for a bit longer than I planned. It was her idea. She doesn't think it's a good idea for me to be living alone with two small children. Especially if you don't come back, but I know you will. You have to. You'll have a son or daughter waiting to meet you. I trust that God will allow you to come home to us. I love you.

Love, Clemmie

May 18, 1965

Dear Julian,

I'm going to be a dad. Clemmie is pregnant, and it's coming in
August. I don't even have the words to describe what I'm
feeling. I'd give my left leg to be back on a plane to New York
right now. I am holding back tears as I write this, knowing
that I can't be there. I might not ever get to meet my kid.
That scares the hell out of me. I would never tell Clemmie
this, but there are times where I'm content with the fact
that I might not make it out of this war. It's my reality, and
I must face that. But knowing that I have a kid on the way
changes everything. I have to get home. I don't have a choice
now. I'm not living for myself anymore. I'm living for my kid.

Love, Danny

May 19, 1965

Dear Clemmie,

I can't believe it. You have no idea how happy this news makes me. I'm so sorry that I can't be there. I'm sorry that I left you, and I want you to know that I will make it back home to my family. I think Sky is a beautiful name. If it's a boy, I want to name him Julian, after my brother. He can have my middle name, of course. I can't wait to see what our baby looks like. If they'll have your eyes or mine. If they'll have my nose, or yours. I hope you're feeling alright and staying healthy. I'm glad you've decided to stay with your grandmother. I don't want you to be alone during your pregnancy or after. My mother's phone number is 555-2368. I've written her a letter, telling her the news, but she'll hear it faster from you. I know she'll be excited. She's always wanted, grandchildren. Maybe when the baby is born, you can visit so that she can meet them. I don't want you to worry about me. I only want you to focus on bringing our healthy baby into this world and taking good care of them and Sunny. Be the best mom that you can be, and in time, we'll all be together again. I love you.

Love, Daniel

June 9, 1965

Dear Mother,

The more time passes, the more nervous I become about having my baby. Daniel is excited and wants to name it after his brother if it's a boy. I think it's a beautiful idea. I miss him so much it hurts. Waking up every day, not knowing if he's alive or dead. I called his mother to tell her about the baby, and she couldn't be happier. We talked for a while and comforted one another with stories about Daniel. She wants me to come down and visit after the baby is born if I can. I told her I would try. If Daniel doesn't make it back, his mother will be all our baby has as a connection to him. I want our child to know who their family is and who their father was. I mean, is. I shouldn't speak of him as if he's already gone. I want our child to learn about their Puerto Rican roots and learn how to speak Spanish. Daniel was supposed to teach me, but we never got around to it. We never got around to a lot of things. But I promise we'll make up for that when he comes home.

I hid my pregnancy from others for the most part. But once my belly got too big to hide, the rumors and nasty remarks began. People have been calling me awful things and calling my baby a bastard child. And a mutt. Not many people know about Daniel, but the neighbors have seen him, so he's never been much of a secret. Some people think I was cheating on Charles during our marriage and that Sunny isn't really his, and it's probably the real reason Charles was killed. When I heard that, I shut everyone out. People can think whatever they want, but I won't be disrespected, and I most certainly won't let anyone disrespect my children. Grandma tells folks to mind their business whenever they ask her questions. I don't know what I would do without her. If you were here, I know you'd have my back too. I miss you, mama. Talk to God for me, and tell him to bring Daniel home safely. Please.

Love, Clemmie

August 12, 1965

Dear Daniel,

You have a son. Julian Ramon Collins-Castillo. Born on August 9th at 8:02 am at Mercy Hospital. Four pounds and six ounces. He's healthy, and he has my eyes. He has your dimples, and your smile. I tried to get a good photo, but it doesn't do him any justice. Just wait until you meet him. Your heart will melt. Mine already has. I've sent photos to your mother as well. I'm doing fine, and we're both at home now. Sunny loves her little brother so much, she's always trying to hold him. As usual, I've been praying for your safe return. I know it's hard, being so far away. But it will all be worth it when you come home. I can't write too much, with two babies and all. But you know I love you, and your son loves you too. We'll be waiting.

Love, Clemmie

September 1, 1965

Dear Julian,

My baby boy is here! Clemmie sent a photo, and I'm in love. I never truly knew what love was until the moment I laid eyes on my son. But after the congrats from my squad, my joy was short-lived. My son is here, and he's almost a month old already. Pretty soon, that month will turn into two, and then six, and before I know it, he'll be a year old. I'll miss his first steps and his first words. I won't be there to feed him when he's hungry or comfort him when he cries. I won't be there to teach him how to speak Spanish or show him how to make Empanadillas. Or teach him how to draw. He won't hear my voice telling him that I love him before he goes to bed at night or when he wakes up in the morning. All I have is this photo, and that's all I might ever get. If I die, I want my son to know, from me, just how much he is loved. So I'm going to write to him, and say all the things my father never could.

Love, Danny

September 1, 1965

Dear Son,

I'm writing you this letter all the way from Vietnam. When your mother told me that she was pregnant with you, I knew at that moment that I was fighting this war for you. Knowing that I have you is what keeps me going every day. By the time you're old enough to understand these words or read them yourself, I may or may not be around. But if I'm not, I want you to know that you are loved. You, Julian Ramon Collins-Castillo, are the light I never knew I needed. The breath that keeps me alive, and just like your mother, you are my dream come true. You saved my life, and I never want you to forget that.

If I am around, then I'm probably reading this letter to you right now, giving you all the love you deserve and more. I hope I am, and I can't wait to watch you grow up and do all the things I couldn't. I love you. *Te Quiero mucho.*

Love, Your father, Daniel
P.S., Did your mother tell you that I was an artist? I drew you a picture. It's called "Watching Over You." I hope you love it.

∞*Part Four*∞

July 9, 1966

Dear Mother,

Daniel's tour in Vietnam is officially over, and he's finally coming home. He arrives in Seattle tomorrow. I haven't heard from Daniel since his last letter that came a few days ago. But it was written almost a month ago, and anything could've happened between then and now. My anxiety has been all over the place. I haven't heard any good news on his whereabouts, but I haven't heard any bad news either, which is still good. Daniel's mother is here, too, spending time with her grandson and waiting for Daniel's arrival. A year and a half since we've seen each other, and it seems like a miracle that we've lasted this long, through dozens of letters, pictures, and prayers. Julian has gotten so big and looks more like his father every day. I can't wait to see him. I can't wait for him to meet his son and for him to see how much Sunny has grown too. I can't wait for us to be a real family finally.

Love Clemmie

July 12, 1966

Dear Little brother,

I want to thank you for guiding me through all these years.
You might not be here physically, but you've been here in
spirit. Giving me an outlet when I had none and being a
shoulder for me when I didn't have one. My time in Vietnam is
over, and I'm home now. With my family, and I never in a
million years imagined happiness such as this. When I arrived
in Seattle, I called Clemmie to tell her I was on my way to
New York. Hearing my voice again, nearly had her in tears.
She put Julian on the phone, and I listened to my son's voice
for the first time. Well, more like muffled sounds. He'll be
one next month. One whole year old. It seems like an
eternity, but I can't change the past. All I can do is look
forward to the future—our future, together.
During my flight to New York, I couldn't get his voice out of
my mind. I was so nervous, afraid that he wouldn't want to
hug me or be around me. I'm still a stranger to him, and it will
take some time for him to get used to me. But I'm prepared,
and so far, it hasn't been so bad.
When I got to Clemmie's house, my heart couldn't take what
stood before me. She was just as beautiful as I
remembered—the love of my life. I didn't even make it to the
door before she came out and threw her arms around me. If
it weren't for Sunny tugging at the hem of her dress, we'd
probably still be in each other's arms. And Sunny, she's so

adorable and has grown so much. Mom was there too, showering me with kisses and thanking Jesus in Spanish. Waiting at the door, hiding behind Grandma Gigi, was my son. I slowly made my way to him as Grandma Gigi pulled him from behind her and told him to say hello. I kneeled, my eyes filling to the brim with tears as I formally introduced myself to him. He was so shy. His eyes hung to the floor. I took his hand. He looked at me and smiled. My baby boy and I still can't believe it. I'm a dad. Our first day together was spent playing with his toys and just watching him be himself. He's in bed now. I stayed with him until he fell asleep in my arms. I don't want to miss a second with him, and I won't.

Clemmie and I plan to move to Florida. She took Julian down there to see mom when he was a few months old. She loved it. I told her we could do whatever she wants. I can apply to school down there and maybe even take Clemmie and the kids to Puerto Rico some time. Mom loves the kids and would like for us to be closer as well. There is so much to look forward to now, and I couldn't be happier. I can't believe it all started with a message in a bottle.

Love, Danny

June 13, 2011

Dear Mother,

Our tradition lives on. It's grandbaby Ashley's 16th birthday, and she's sending out her letter today. She's not as excited as Sunny and Julian were at her age, but if I've done one thing right, it's taught my children and grandchildren the importance of tradition. Julian and his wife are working, and Sunny is at her son's graduation. So it's just Daniel and me, on the beach with Ashley as she prepares to release her letter out into the world. This is the same beach where Daniel found my letter too. The kids have always loved the story of how we met. It's one of the things that keeps the tradition alive. The story of a love that stood the test of time, distance, doubt, and even war. Through it all, we have each other, and what a blessed journey it has been.

Love, Clemmie

June 13, 2011

Dear Person, (Whoever you are)

If you're reading this, then that means my letter actually survived the rough waters of the ocean and found you. My name is Ashley Castillo, and it's my 16th birthday. It's a family tradition to put messages in bottles and send them out in hopes that some stranger will find it and bring them good luck. I think it's kinda lame, but you never know. My grandma said I should put my address on here, but that's weird, so I won't. This isn't the 50's. You can email me at kweenashley@gmail.com or follow me on Twitter @kweenashleyc.
Whoever you are, I hope the sun shined for you today. I hope you're cute (kidding), and I hope this letter finds you well.

With Love, Ashley C.

"Love recognizes no barriers. It jumps hurdles, leaps fences, penetrates walls to arrive at its destination full of hope."
-Maya Angelou

Thank you for reading!
Don't forget to leave a review on amazon or Goodreads!
Check out these other books by Chanel!

Fernando
My Colorblind Rainbow
River's Moonlight
The Coldest Moon
The Harvest Moon: A Prequel
Was It Her?
Mahogany Tales
I Had A Dream About You: A Collection of Poems
Sweet Oleander: A Collection of Poetry

Also Follow me on social media @chanelhardypub_

About the Author

Born and raised in the Washington D.C. area, writing has been a passion of mine since I was young. I started writing my first book, 'My Colorblind Rainbow' in 2013. In 2017, I decided to continue writing, taking a leap of faith and following my dreams of publishing my first book which made the 'In The Margins Award Long List' for YA fiction in 2018. I launched Hardy Publications in September of 2017, working as a freelance writer and literary blogger. I've written for publications such as Women and Words, 25 Hottest Indie Authors Artists Advocates 2020, and CulEpi. With certifications in persuasive writing and public speaking, TEFL(Teaching English as a Foreign Language) while overseas, I use my platform to raise awareness for different charities and non-profit organizations, volunteering both locally and internationally, and donating a portion of my platform's earnings to help others in need.

www.ingramcontent.com/pod-product-compliance
Lightning Source LLC
Chambersburg PA
CBHW052001170626
46808CB00007B/2729